BLUE FROG

The Legend of Chocolate

By Dianne
de Las Casas

Illustrated by
Holly Stone-Barker

PELICAN PUBLISHING COMPANY

Gretna 2011

To Lisa Jacob, a true
blue friend! I love you!
—Dianne de Las Casas

To my mom, for the wisdom and
richness you bring to my life.
—Holly Stone-Barker

Library of Congress
Cataloging-in-Publication Data

De las Casas, Dianne.
  Blue frog : the legend of chocolate / Dianne de Las Casas ; illustrated by Holly Stone-Barker.
    p. cm.
  ISBN 978-1-4556-1459-2 (hardcover : alk. paper)
  1. Aztecs—Folklore. 2. Aztec mythology—Juvenile literature. 3. Cacao beans—Juvenile
literature. 4. Chocolate—Juvenile literature. 5. Tales—Mexico. 6. Legends—Mexico. I.
Stone-Barker, Holly. II. Title. III. Title: Legend of chocolate.
  F1219.76.F65D4 2011
  398.2089'974—dc23

                    2011013000

Printed in Singapore
Published by Pelican Publishing Company, Inc.
1000 Burmaster Street, Gretna, Louisiana 70053

Sun God smiled as he looked at *su tesoro,* his treasure, on the banks of the Great Pond. It was *el árbol de cacao,* the cacao tree, from which cacao pods grew. Hidden inside the pod was the secret food of the gods, the cacao bean.

Every day Sun God enjoyed his cacao. Rich and dark, he savored its flavor. *"Mmmm. ¡Delicioso!"* he remarked as he ate. "Delicious!"

Nearby, Wind God watched as Sun God devoured the cacao. "So that is where he keeps his cacao," Wind God said.

Wind God approached Sun God. "You should share your *tesoro de cacao,* your cacao treasure, with the people of the earth."

Sun God laughed. "This is the food of the gods. I will never share."

Wind God replied, "Earth's people deserve to taste the divine."

Wind God left and transformed himself into *una rana azul,* a blue frog. He hid near the banks of Great Pond and watched as Sun God scraped the cacao from inside the pod. Rana Azul said, "If Sun God will not share his treasure, I will tell Earth's people about it."

"Rrrrrrreeeeeep.

Rana Azul sat by the edge of the pond
near *los niños*, the children, and sang,

"Rrrrrreeeeep. Rrrrrreeeeeep.

Sun God hides his treasure deep.
By the pond, inside large pods,
he hides the secret food of gods."

Los niños heard *el canción de* Rana Azul,
the song of Blue Frog. They ran to their village.

"Lo-a, lo-a,

lo-a, lo-a, lo-a,"

"Rrrrrreeeeep.

Rrrrrreeeeep."

Los niños returned with their mothers and
pointed to Rana Azul. He sang again,

"Rrrrrreeeeep. Rrrrrreeeeep.

Sun God hides his treasure deep.
By the pond, inside large pods,
he hides the secret food of gods."

Los niños and their mothers heard
el canción de Rana Azul. They ran to their village.

"Lo-a, lo-a,

lo-a, lo-a, lo-a."

"Rrrrrreeeeep.

Rrrrrreeeeep."

Los niños returned with their mothers and
pointed to Rana Azul. He sang again,

"Rrrrrreeeeep. Rrrrrreeeeeep.

Sun God hides his treasure deep.
By the pond, inside large pods,
he hides the secret food of gods."

Listening to *el canción de* Rana Azul, Earth's people began searching for *el tesoro.* They found *un árbol grande,* a large tree, next to the Great Pond. Near the trunk of the tree lay several large pods. Upon opening the pods, they discovered the delicious, secret food of the gods, the cacao bean.

Sun God was

Furious,

but there was nothing he could do.
His secret was now known to all of
Earth's people.

The people delighted in the rich taste of the cacao bean. They exclaimed, *"¡Delicioso!"* They cultivated the seeds and grew more trees. They named the tasty, dark substance from the cacao bean "cacahuatl." Today, we know this *comida divina,* or divine food, as "chocolate."

Author's Note

This book was inspired by a local chocolate shop in New Orleans, Louisiana, called Blue Frog Chocolates, owned by Ann and Rick Streiffer. They named their shop after the legend of the blue frog. I love chocolate in its many forms. I have seen a live cacao pod, crunched on cocoa nibs, and even toured a real chocolate factory. My favorite book in the whole world is *Charlie and the Chocolate Factory!* I also adore the country of Mexico and visit when I can. Holly did a tremendous amount of research in depicting the art for this book. She works in cut-paper and collage, often hand-painting her paper to achieve a particular texture. The vivid colors and lines of Aztec and Mayan art inspired her. Of course, we both had tons of fun doing our research because we *had* to eat lots of CHOCOLATE!

Mexican Hot Cocoa

The Aztec people learned to make a hot drink using the cacao bean. We know this drink as hot cocoa. The Aztecs used chile in their hot cocoa. When the Conquistadors brought cacao back to Spain, sugar was added to the drink. Try this delicious recipe, which combines the best of both worlds. If you like your cocoa sweet, without spice, omit the chile powder. If you want it rich, substitute boiling milk for the boiling water.

Ingredients:
3 tsp. cocoa powder
1 tsp. vanilla
4 tsp. brown sugar
2/3 cup boiling water
Chile or chipotle powder, to taste

Directions:
Place cocoa powder, vanilla, and brown sugar in a mug. Pour in boiling water. Mix thoroughly. Add a dash of chile powder and mix. Let cool. Enjoy! *¡Delicioso!*